T0193536

Mumford Saves the World

A Rescue Dog Diary

Author: Jeff Moulton
Illustrator: Nafeesa Arshad

AuthorHouse™
1663 Liberty Drive
Bloomington, IN 47403
www.authorhouse.com
Phone: 833-262-8899

Because of the dynamic nature of the Internet, any web addresses or links contained in this book may have changed since publication and may no longer be valid. The views expressed in this work are solely those of the author and do not necessarily reflect the views of the publisher, and the publisher hereby disclaims any responsibility for them.

This book is printed on acid-free paper.

ISBN: 979-8-8230-1965-1 (sc)
ISBN: 979-8-8230-1966-8 (hc)
ISBN: 979-8-8230-1967-5 (e)

Library of Congress Control Number: 2023924414

Print information available on the last page.

Published by AuthorHouse 01/11/2024

authorHOUSE

Hi!

My name is Mumford, and I am a superhero!

Well, honestly, I am just a really great dog who got a second chance.

My parents are the ones who call me a superhero-most days, anyway.

I want to tell my story because maybe I can help more humans think about all the great things dogs are capable of every day.

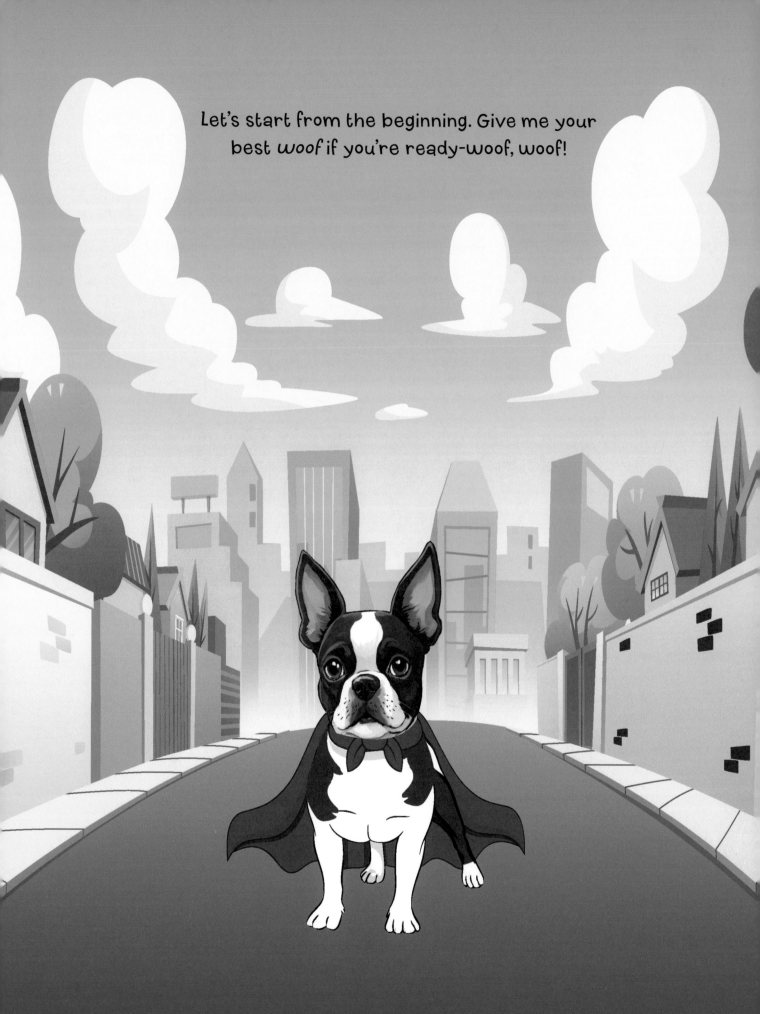

Let's start from the beginning. Give me your best *woof* if you're ready-woof, woof!

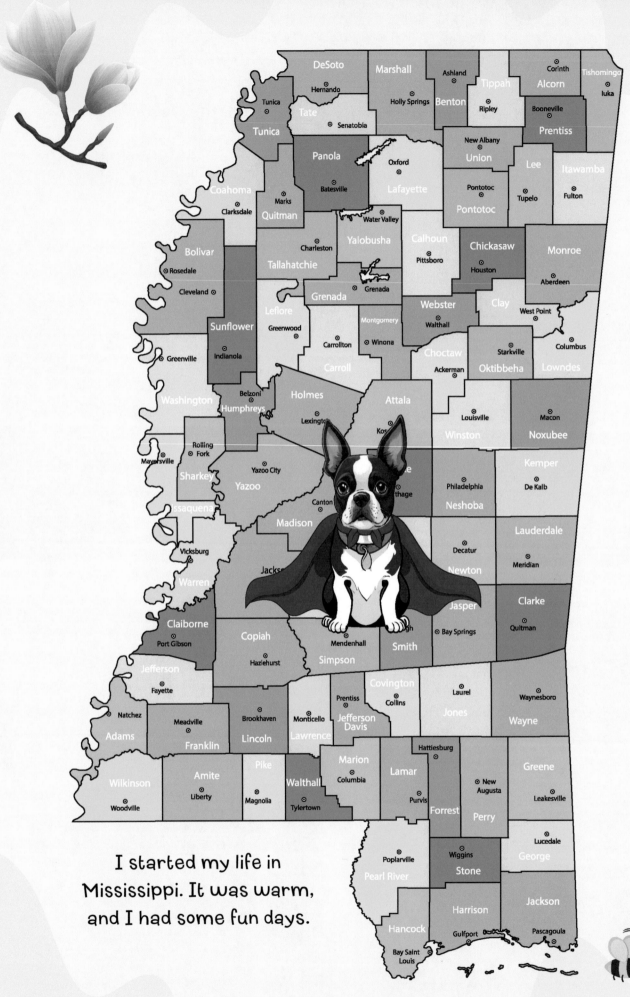

I started my life in
Mississippi. It was warm,
and I had some fun days.

4

Unfortunately, after a few years, my family had to move away, and I became a stray. It was cool at first; I was able to be outside, roam the streets, and play with my friends. The only problem was I didn't really have a home. I wandered a lot, I missed my family, and no one loved me. I was lonely and scared most days.

After roaming the streets for a while, I had an accident. It wasn't like pooping on the carpet, which we dogs sometimes do by mistake. This was a big one!

I got hit by a truck because I wasn't looking both ways when I crossed the street. Trust me-Mumford the superhero-it is *very important* to look both ways when you cross the street.

It was then that my life changed, and I became the superhero that I am today.

We love all dogs rescue

A rescue made up of some pretty amazing humans who love all dogs took me in and gave me the care I needed to get better. I had to go to a doctor to fix my wounds, and I was there for a while.

My rescue humans helped me through everything, and after I got done healing, it was time to find my forever home. No more streets for this guy!

This is when things got *really cool!*

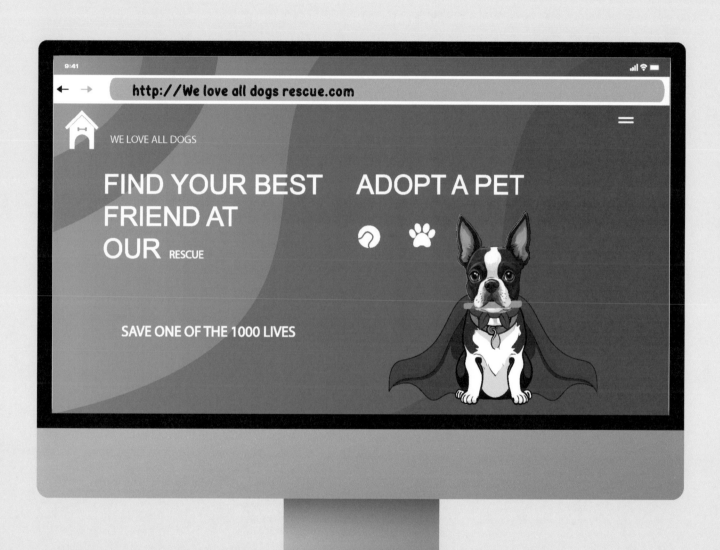

My amazingly handsome face was put on the rescue organization's website, with a story about what the rescue humans knew about me. They knew I was healthy now and that I loved my toys. I always had a toy with me.

After a few weeks, my life changed forever. One day the phone rang at the rescue, and it was someone calling about me!

That someone was, my adoptive dad and he had been accepted by the rescue to adopt me! I was over the Moon! Woohoo, I was going to my forever home! But wait-I didn't even know what that meant. I had so many questions.

Where was I going? Who was this new dad the rescue humans seemed excited about? Would I have brothers and sisters? Would I be able to make new friends? I was scared!

Soon after that, it was time for me to be transported. I don't like cars, and I especially don't like big scary trucks for obvious reasons. I just told myself, *Remember, Mumford, you are a superhero.*

Pawsitively Awesome Transport

The next day I got on the transport, and we were off.
I got to my next stop just fine, but where was I?

Pawsitively Awesome Transport

I didn't know at the time, but turned out I went from Mississippi to Maine, where my new adoptive family lived. I got carried off the transport, and oh man, superhero or not, it was cold. Brrr!

For a few days, I stayed with a foster family to make sure I was healthy. I felt pretty good and was excited about what was to come.

After that first few days in Maine, my foster mom came into the room, woke me up, and said, "Mumford, it's time to get you ready; you are going to your forever home today!"

I was excited and nervous. We traveled a short distance by car to meet my new mom and dad.

Then, the car stopped, and it was time. The door opened, and I gulped really hard and reminded myself ...

Mumford, you are a superhero.
Mumford, you are a superhero.
Mumford, you are a superhero.

And then, my forever dad appeared. He was big and tall, he had a friendly smile, and he reached into the car calmly and took me out. I'll never forget what he said in his big, tall voice.

"Nice to meet you, Mumford. I'm your new dad. Everything is going to be A-OK, and we are going to have lots of fun. You are a very special boy!"

We walked over to his car, and I got to meet my mom. Oh my, she was so sweet, like moms usually are.

She immediately got a bed ready in the back of the car and prepared a blanket. She went right into mom mode and got me my favorite toy. I love toys!

The ride home was short, thankfully, because I was so excited.
On my way there, my dad told me I had a teenage brother
(he was human), and an older sister, who looked a lot like
me. I was getting wiggle butt just thinking about it.

We arrived home to a really cool house made of brick. We went inside to see my new home. Do you know who met me at the door?

My sister-or, as my dad likes to call her, Queen Farty Pants!
Her real name is Gabby, and she is a Boston terrier, just like me.
My mom and dad also rescued her.

This might have been the greatest day ever!

Mom and Dad showed me the house. It was definitely dog friendly, with blankets and toys and furniture I could sit on and sleep on. Gabby showed me the ropes. She said, "This is all ours. We run this place!"

After we walked around the house, there was another surprise: a big yard, all fenced in for us. It was huge! Holy cowabunga! I could run my zoomies anytime I wanted now, as fast as I wanted, whenever I wanted. Do you do zoomies? If not, you should try; they're easy. I run as fast as I can in one direction, and then I run back! It's so much fun. I do zoomies as often as I can, but almost always do them after I do my poops at night.

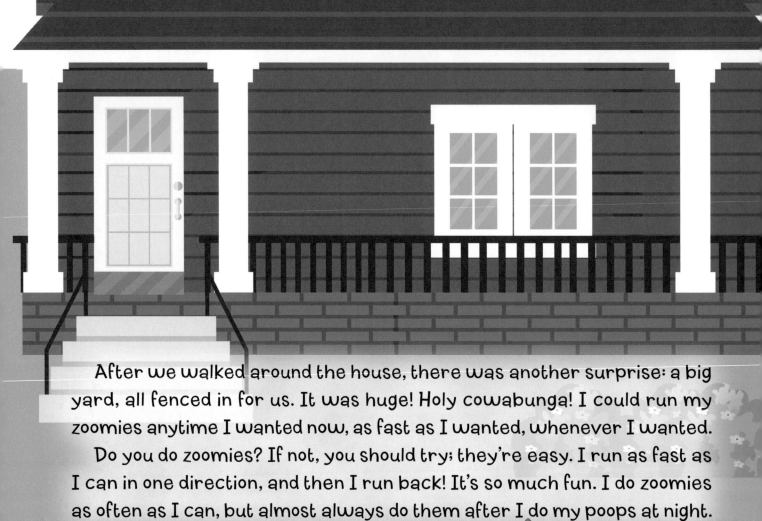

After a little while of getting to know my new home, I found out I had one more surprise.

My Brother! He was young and loved to play with me all the time. I loved him so much and got super excited when he got home. (Well, I got super excited when anyone got home.) His name was Alden, and he came home from school. He was just as excited to see me as I was to see him.

At this point, I was feeling pretty
dang thankful for my second chance.
This was gonna be awesome!

It has been two years since I moved to Maine, and I could not be happier. Here's my superhero day!

I wake up, have breakfast, go on an adventure walk with my dad, come home, eat, take a poop, and take a nap in my favorite place, the blanket basket. Then I get up, do a double stretch, go pee, and then take another nap. And by then my mom and dad are just about home from work!

I greet them at the door, excited as always. Then, it's adventure time again! We eat and then snuggle on the couch, and if I'm lucky, Dad will play tug-of-war with me. It's my favorite game in the whole universe! I let my dad win sometimes.

I have a great life, thanks to some really great people.
My family is always there, and now, most important,
I know in my heart that this is my forever home.

I wanted to share my story with you because maybe today wasn't so great, but tomorrow might be better; I promise! When you help others-dogs, humans, or anything else-

You can be a superhero, just like me!

Printed in the United States
by Baker & Taylor Publisher Services